6/62

AT

HOUND HOTEL

PICTURE WINDOW BOOKS
A Capstone Imprint

Adventures at Hound Hotel is published by Picture Window Books,
a Capstone imprint
1710 Roe Crest Drive
North Mankato, Minnesota 56003
www.mycapstone.com

Library of Congress Cataloging-in-Publication Data
Names: Sateren, Shelley Swanson, author. | Melmon, Deborah, illustrator. | Sateren,
Shelley Swanson. Adventures at Hound Hotel.
Title: Drooling Dudley / by Shelley Swanson Sateren; [illustrated by Deborah Melmon].
Description: North Mankato, Minnesota: Picture Window Books, a Capstone imprint,
[2017] | Series: Adventures at Hound Hotel | Summary: Alfie Wolfe is a lot messier than
his twin sister, Alfreeda, but he may have met his match in Dudley, an English bulldog
with a serious drool problem—and it is up to Alfie to care for and clean up after him
at the Hound Hotel.
Identifiers: LCCN 2016012619 | ISBN 9781515802204 (library binding) |
ISBN 9781515802228 (paperback) | ISBN 9781515802242 (eBook (pdf))
Subjects: LCSH: Bulldog—Juvenile fiction. | Dogs—Juvenile fiction. | Kennels—
Juvenile fiction. | Cleaning—Juvenile fiction. | Twins—Juvenile fiction. | Brothers
and sisters—Juvenile fiction. | CYAC: Bulldog—Fiction. | Dogs—Fiction. | Kennels—
Fiction. | Cleanliness—Fiction. | Twins—Fiction. | Brothers and sisters—Fiction.
Classification: LCC PZ7.S249155 Dr 2017 | DDC 813.54—dc23
LC record available at http://lccn.loc.gov/2016012619

Designer: Heidi Thompson

Drooling Dudley

by Shelley Swanson Sateren
illustrated by Deborah Melmon

TABLE OF CONTENTS

ADVENTURES AT HOUND HOTEL

IT'S TIME FOR YOUR ADVENTURE AT HOUND HOTEL!

At Hound Hotel, dogs are given the royal treatment. We are a top-notch boarding kennel. When your dog stays with us, we will follow your feeding schedule, give them walks, and tuck them in at night.

We are always just a short walk away from the dogs — the kennels are located in a heated building at the end of our driveway. Every dog has his or her own pen, with a bed, blanket, and water dish.

Rest assured . . . a stay at the Hound Hotel is like a vacation for your dog. We have a large play yard, plenty of toys, and pool time in the summer. Your dog will love playing with the other guests.

HOUND HOTEL
WHO'S WHO

WINIFRED WOLFE

Hound Hotel is run by Winifred Wolfe, a lifelong dog lover. Winifred loves dogs of all sorts. She wants to spend time with every breed. When she's not taking care of the canines, she writes books about — you guessed it — dogs.

ALFIE AND ALFREEDA WOLFE

Winifred's young twins help out as much as they can. Whether your dog needs gentle attention or extra playtime, Alfreeda and Alfie provide special services you can't find anywhere else. Your dog will never get bored with these two on the job.

WOLFGANG WOLFE

Winifred's husband pitches in at the hotel whenever he can, but he spends much of his time traveling to study wolf packs. Wolfgang is a real wolf lover — he even named his children after pack leaders, the alpha wolves. Every wolf pack has two alpha wolves: a male one and a female one, just like the Wolfe family twins.

Next time your family goes on vacation, bring your dog to Hound Hotel.

Your pooch is sure to have a howling good time!

CHAPTER 1
Alpha Mess-Maker

I'm Alfie Wolfe, and there's one thing I hate: cleaning.

It's boring. I'm bad at it. And it's a HUGE waste of time.

Here's the thing . . . I *like* things messy. I *like* my stuff all over the place. I don't *want* to put my skateboard away every night. I might need it quick the next morning, for Pete's sake.

But this story isn't about how much I avoid cleaning. Well, not totally. It's about a messy dog named Dudley. A bulldog, to be exact. An English bulldog, to be exacter. The alpha mess-maker of the dog world, to be exactest. ("Alpha" means "first" or "top.")

I think Dudley and I tied in mess-making skills. I'm not bragging, but creating messes comes real natural to me. I hardly try, and messes just happen.

Cleaning them up, though? That's hard.

Nope, I will never, ever measure up in the wipe-things-down department. Or in the keeping-things-spotless-and-neat department. Not compared to my twin sister, Alfreeda. She's the alpha kid in those areas.

Well, fine. She can have the honor.

But back to Dudley. He and I had lots in common. Mostly this: We made messes and expected other people to clean them up.

It all started one super-hot August morning. I couldn't wait to meet Dudley. We'd never had an English bulldog stay at our dog hotel before. A *French* bulldog had visited once, but French bulldogs are littler, with perky, bat-like ears.

I was sitting on the living room floor, watching TV and eating cereal. Just killing time before Dudley arrived. The TV show was called *Mister Muttley's Magic Hour*. A show for little kids about a crazy terrier that does magic tricks.

Suddenly my mom and sister came tearing down the stairs. I jumped. The milk in my bowl splashed over the edge and spilled on the rug. I quickly moved in front of the mess so Mom wouldn't notice.

The two of them were dressed for the workday in the dog kennels. They wore matching jeans and Hound Hotel T-shirts.

They stopped halfway across the living room and looked at the bottom of their shoes.

"Oh, Alfie," Mom sighed. "You still haven't wiped up the juice you spilled yesterday. Now my shoes are all sticky again."

"Mine too," Alfreeda complained.

"Sorry," I said. I kept staring at the TV.

Mom marched over and stood in front of the TV. "Alfie, what's wrong with this picture?" she asked me.

"Nothing," I said. "The show's coming in nice and clear. The new antennae Dad put on the roof works great."

"Not the TV picture," Mom said. She waved her arm. "This! This room! Look! It's full of your messes."

"Mine?" I cried. "How about hers?" I pointed at my sister.

Alfreeda laughed and rolled her eyes. "Yeah, right," she said.

"Alfie," Mom said in her I-mean-business voice, "I've spent too much time cleaning up your messes. I almost wiped up your spilled juice last night, but I stopped myself. From now on, if *you* make a mess, *you* clean it up.

Don't come out to the kennels until this living room is spotless!"

"But, Mom!" I said, jumping up. "Dudley's coming! This is my first chance to hang out with an English bulldog."

Mom pointed at the floor. "What's that wet spot on the rug?" she asked.

"Milk," I answered.

"Clean it up," she said. "Alfreeda, let's go. We've got a busy day ahead of us."

They hurried out the back door.

I looked around the room and groaned. Then I started to complain out loud. "This will take *all day*! I'll *never* get to do fun stuff with Dudley. HELP!"

No one answered. No one in the whole world heard my cry for help. Not even my dad, the one person who might understand my point of view. (He was up north again, studying wolves. That's his job.)

Actually, Dad would probably be on Mom's side. He likes stuff neat . . . and not sticky.

Truth is, I am a lone wolf in the Wolfe family. The only one who likes things messy. It can get lonesome sometimes.

I studied the living room. Man, I'd really made a mess of things this time. Here's what I saw: piles of photos Dad had sent me from wolf country; a bunch of funny stuff I'd printed off the Internet; spilled popcorn; half-eaten apples; banana peels; dirty socks and T-shirts; dirty dishes and glasses. . . .

I sighed, real heavy. I didn't know where to start.

But then I got an idea. A great one.

I'll make up a magic spell, I thought. *One that makes messes disappear. If a tiny dog like Mister Muttley can do magic, then so can I!*

I thought for a minute. Then I said these words out loud, in a deep, full-of magic voice:

Magic helpers, please appear.

Come out from the fog.

Make this big mess disappear.

Take pity on Alfie-dog!

I held my breath and spun in a fast circle.

I couldn't believe what happened next.

— CHAPTER 2 —
Magic Cleaning Spell

The back door banged open. Someone ran through the kitchen. Had a magic helper come to save me?

I had no idea what a magic helper coming out of the fog would look like. And the weird thing was, the sun burned bright that morning. There wasn't a bit of fog anywhere. But I was ready! I needed help!

Suddenly Alfreeda leaped into the doorway between the kitchen and the living room.

"Not you," I said with a groan. "Some magic."

"Huh?" Alfreeda said. Her face wrinkled up. "You're weird, Alfie Wolfe."

"You're weirder, Alfreeda Wolfe," I said.

"Hey, Mom said she needs you at the kennel building now, not later. The hotel is overbooked. Tons of guests. She needs us both to help, on the double."

"What?" I said. "For real?"

Alfreeda nodded.

"Yes!" I pounded the air above my head. "Is Dudley here yet?"

Alfreeda nodded again. "Mom wants you to care for him *all day*. She said you can clean the living room tonight."

"You bet I will!" I said.

"I bet you won't," she said.

"Will too."

"Will not."

"Whatever," I said. "This is so great!" I found a pair of dirty socks on the floor and tugged them on. I found my shoes under the couch and tugged those on too. "What dog did you pick to play with?" I asked.

"I didn't. I have to vacuum the kennels," Alfreeda said. "A lot of shedding dogs stayed last night."

I stared at my sister. *Something's wrong with this picture*, I thought. *Why wasn't she complaining? Why wasn't she stamping her foot? This deal was totally unfair. I get to hang out with Dudley all day, but she has to vacuum all the dog pens?*

I covered my mouth to hide a grin. This was some kind of crazy magic at work. Thank you, Mister Muttley!

Well, you can bet I wasn't going to point out the unfairness. I kept my mouth shut and headed for the doorway.

I marched toward my sister and realized something very cool: Turning your back on a big mess makes it totally disappear. Man, I liked magic.

I pushed past Alfreeda and raced to the kennel building. She raced after me.

For once I beat my sister to the office door. I threw it open and called, "Hey, Dudley! It's Alfie, here to give you a rocking good time. Let's get this party started! How about some Frisbee in the big play yard? You're going to love it out there! You can see the lake, the woods, and the farm animals next door.

We'll spend all day outside, having a blast! Just you and me on this great summer day!"

Alfreeda walked past me and laughed.

It was her that's-what-you-think laugh.

That's when I realized that Alfreeda knew something I didn't. Something about Dudley the bulldog.

Uh-oh.

⟩—CHAPTER 3 —⟨
The Spit Monster

I tore through the office, down the hallway, and past the storeroom.

"Mom!" I yelled. "Mom! Where are you? Where's Dudley?"

"Back here," she called.

Her voice came from the back of the building. It's where all the dog pens are.

(Or you can call them kennels. Take your pick. You can even call them runs, if you want. Each run is big enough for a dog to *run* around inside. Get it?)

I ducked into the kennel room, and the loud place got even louder. A bunch of dogs barked their heads off at me.

"Hey, everybody!" I said with a wave.

Each of the twelve pens had a dog in it. Terriers. Beagles. Golden retrievers. Labradors. All kinds of mixes too.

Then I spotted Dudley. You couldn't miss him. He had a big square head and a big wide body on top of short, skinny legs.

He had a pushed-in face and loose, wrinkly skin all over it. He had little ears too. And an under bite. That means his lower jaw stuck out.

I ran over to his pen and waved at him.

"Hey, Dudley Old Boy," I said. "We're going to hang out together. We can play catch in the play yard all day long!"

He wagged his stump of a tail and woofed.

"He likes me, Mom," I said.

"Of course he does," she said. She smiled and pressed a wet cloth on Dudley's neck. "But this friendly guy can't play outside today, I'm afraid."

"Huh?" I said. "How come?"

"It's too hot, Alfie. Bulldogs are indoor dogs. Their short, flat noses make it hard for them to breathe and cool down. They can't stand the heat. It's really unsafe for them. I'm finally getting Dudley cooled down after his short walk from the car to the kennel. Maybe after the sun sets, he can have a very short walk up the road."

"Aww, Mom," I groaned. "Really?"

"Sorry, Alfie. He has to stay inside, in the air-conditioned building. You can play with him in the office when Alfreeda vacuums the pens. Dudley's new-visitor form said that vacuum cleaners make him nervous. And when he's nervous, he drools even more. I know, it's hard to believe he could drool *more*, but . . ."

That's when I saw the long white strings of drool hanging out the sides of Dudley's mouth.

"Wow, he's a spit monster," I said.

"Mm-hmm," Mom agreed. "That's normal for a bulldog."

I headed inside Dudley's pen and patted the smooth fur on his back. He shook his head back and forth real fast. A waterfall of drool flew from his mouth and got all over my face, neck, and T-shirt.

"Cool! He totally slimed me, Mom," I said. "That's so awesome!"

Mom laughed. "You two messy guys are going to get along great."

"We sure are." I hugged Dudley around his big, strong shoulders.

"Speaking of messes," Mom said, pointing at the corner of the pen. "See that?"

"What?" All I saw was an empty water bowl and a bunch of water on the floor around it.

"Dudley did that," Mom said. "Bulldogs are messy drinkers because of all the loose skin around their mouths. They can't close their teeth, jaws, or lips tightly enough to keep water inside."

"Or their spit," I said.

"That's right. So, Alfie," Mom went on, "you've got two important jobs today. First, keep Dudley nice and cool by getting him lots of fresh water."

"Got it. What's the second thing?"

"Wipe up the floor after him right away, every time he has a drink," Mom said. "It's not safe to have wet floors anywhere in the building. Okay?"

"Okay," I said.

Mom stared at me.

"What?" I asked.

"Well, go get a towel," she said. "Wipe up the water. Now, not later."

"Okay," I said with a sigh. I went to the storeroom and grabbed a towel. I dug in the toy boxes and grabbed a beach ball, a softball, and a Frisbee too.

I got back to the kennel room just as Alfreeda dragged the vacuum cleaner out of the closet.

"Where's Mom?" I asked.

"She took the biggest shedders for a walk," Alfreeda said. "I'm supposed to vacuum their pens while they're gone."

"Well, in that case . . ." I threw open Dudley's gate and dropped the towel inside his pen. "No time to wipe up the water right now. Mom'll understand. If the vacuum cleaner makes the old boy nervous, then I've got to get him out of here. Come on, Dudley. Look what I've got!"

I showed him the toys. He woofed, wagged his tail, and followed me out of the kennel.

"Mom put a pail of water in the office for Dudley," Alfreeda said. "And towels. She said you're supposed to wipe up his drinking messes right away, so no one wipes out."

I'm not bragging, but I'm real skilled at tuning out my sister. So I pretended I didn't hear and led Dudley to the office.

"This way, boy," I said, shutting the office door behind us. "How about tossing the beach ball around first, okay? It'll be just like a fun day at the beach, I promise."

Dudley woofed. Drool dripped on the floor.

"No problem," I said. "We all . . . um . . . drool when we're excited, right?"

I had no idea that Dudley would soon create an *ocean* of drool at our indoor beach party. And a sea of other stuff — liquid *and* solid.

The fun lasted a grand total of two minutes.

CHAPTER 4
Pool of Drool

Down the hall, Alfreeda turned on the vacuum cleaner.

Even though the office door was closed, the noise made more drool drip out of Dudley's mouth. Long, white strings made little pools by his front paws.

"Just pretend that dumb vacuum cleaner isn't there, okay?" I said. "Come on, let's play ball. There's nothing like a good game of catch to calm a person down. Or a dog. Ready? Set? Here comes!"

I tossed the beach ball to Dudley. It bounced off the top of his head and shot back at me. I mean, *straight* back at me.

"Wow, you've got great aim, Dudley," I said. "Do that again!"

I tossed the ball a second time. Get this: My *aim* was off, but Dudley stepped sideways to meet the ball head on. But that's not all. He tipped his head back real quick. The ball bounced off the top of his head and flew high in the air.

"Man, who taught you to do that?" I cried.

The ball sailed way up, then came straight down, right into my arms. Catching it was the easiest thing I've ever done.

"You're a pro!" I said. "This is so cool. Ready? Here it comes again."

But when I tossed the ball this time, Dudley turned. He headed for the water bucket.

The ball bounced off Mom's desk and rolled into a corner. Dudley walked right past it, leaving a river of spit behind him.

He stuck his face in the water and drank like he'd walked through the desert and was dying of thirst. When he was done, he shook his head back and forth. Super fast.

Water and spit splashed everywhere — all over Mom's desk, the floor, the wall, the chairs, and the front door.

At that moment the doorbell rang. It sounds like a barking dog: *Yip! Yip! Yip!*

The sound made Dudley go totally crazy. He barked super loud, then ran to the couch.

He jumped onto it and looked out the big window. He had a good view of the front steps.

The door swung open, and Brianne stepped inside. She's the lady who brings dog food to our kennel every week.

"Hey, Alfie, my man," she said.

"Hey, Brianne," I said.

She carried a huge bag of dog food over her shoulder. She's super strong.

"Who's this guy?" she said real loud over Dudley's barking. "A bulldog! I love bulldogs. Shhh, now, it's okay."

Dudley quieted down.

"His name is Dudley," I said. "He's friendly, gentle, *and* a great ball player."

"I am not surprised," Brianne said. "But I think that vacuum cleaner is making him drool.

It's upsetting you, isn't it, Dudley? How about a back rub? That'll calm you down."

I pointed at the wet floor. "Uh, Brianne, watch your —"

Too late.

Before I had a chance to say "step," Brianne took one step toward Dudley and totally wiped out in the pool of drool.

Her feet and legs shot forward. Her head and arms shot backward. The bag of dog food slid off her shoulder.

"Yikes!" she yelled.

Then she and the dog food crash-landed on the office floor. *THUD! THUD!*

CHAPTER 5

Lake Spit-and-Splash

Brianne sat up and slowly rubbed the back of her head. She closed her eyes and wrinkled her forehead.

I know pain when I see it. My head kind of hurt too, just watching Brianne rub her own. I'd seen the whole wipeout. Her head had hit the seat of a chair.

"I'm real sorry, Brianne," I said. "Does it hurt a lot?"

"Kind of, kiddo," she said in a weak voice. "I'm feeling foggy in the brain at the moment."

"Oh, man," I said. "Don't worry about carrying the dog-food bag to the storeroom. Alfreeda and I will drag it there later."

Brianne tried to get up but sat right back down. She leaned against the desk. The bag lay in the middle of Lake Spit-and-Splash like a big, brown island.

Brianne's as powerful as a Rottweiler. I'd known her my whole life. Never once had I seen her woozy. But she looked pretty woozy right now.

"I should've wiped up Dudley's mess," I said. "I didn't have time. You came in the door so fast. I'm sorry, Brianne. I'm going to go get my mom and —"

"Wait, wait, wait," Brianne said. "Slow down. I'll be fine. I just need to sit a minute."

"I think I better get Mom," I said.

And that's when I got hit in the head by . . . dog food?

"Oh, no!" I cried.

Small, round, hard pieces of dog food started flying through the air, in all directions. They went *PING! PING! PING!* on the glass windows and metal desk. They bounced off the walls and framed pictures of dogs. They covered the floor.

"Dudley, stop!" I cried.

Dudley had ripped a huge hole in the bag. He was chewing a mouthful of food and digging through the rest with all four paws. Like a terrier digging in garden dirt.

His paws were lightning fast. They shot the hard pieces of dog food through the air. Some hit my arms. Some hit my legs. A few hit my face. Brianne's too.

It was like a painful, powerful dog food storm. And I was right in the center of it.

"Ow!" I cried. "Dudley, cut it out!"

— CHAPTER 6 —
Dog Food Battlefield

Dudley acted like he couldn't hear a word I said.

"Hey, you," I said over the loud *PINGS* of dog food. "I know when someone pretends not to hear directions. I do it to my mom all the time. So listen up. Cut that out!"

Well, he kept right on shooting dog food all over the room.

I leaped over and tried to tug Dudley away from the bag. But he was big and heavy, and I couldn't move him.

"Alfreeda!" I yelled.

She appeared in a hot second. She took one look at me, Brianne, and the mess, and said, "Mom is going to be SO mad."

"Don't just stand there," I said. "Help me get Dudley to his pen!"

"Okay, okay," she said. "But we better help Brianne first!"

Brianne shook her head. "I'm fine, kiddo. Help your brother. I'm just catching my breath over here."

Alfreeda dived into action. Together we tried to drag Drooling Dudley away from the bag. He rode it like a surfboard across the room, cutting wakes in the sea of dog food.

"Let's try to lift him," I suggested.

My sister and I huffed and puffed. We tried
to lift that heavy guy off the paper-bag island.
But no luck. Our shoes kept sliding on dog
food or slipping on drool.

I was panting like a bulldog on a hot day. "I need a break," I said.

"Me too," Alfreeda said.

We sat on the floor next to Dudley. He kept right on eating.

"Seeing all this food is making him drool even more," Brianne said. She leaned over and pushed some pieces away from him.

"He's not supposed to eat that much either," Alfreeda said. "He's overweight. His owners want him to lose a few pounds."

"How do you know that?" I asked.

"I read it. On his new-visitor form. It's on Mom's desk. It's got a lot of good information about this crazy old dog."

I jumped up. I couldn't let my sister know more about Dudley than I did.

As I crossed the room to the desk, my shoes crushed the dog food to bits. The place looked like a battlefield. Dog food lay everywhere — in plants, on shelves, under chairs. . . .

I found the new-visitor form and picked up the water bucket. Pieces of dog food floated on top of the water.

I set the bucket in front of Dudley's nose.

"You're hot and thirsty after all that digging, aren't you, boy?" I asked.

He didn't answer. Not just because he's a dog and can't talk. But because he was already too busy drinking.

Dudley stuck his whole face in the water, then raised his head and looked away. Water dripped all over the rug and floor. He did that again and again and again. He made a whole new lake.

Then he lifted his chin and shook his head back and forth super fast. He totally slimed my sister.

"Hey!" Alfreeda yelled, wiping her face with her T-shirt. "I hope that was just water and not dog spit."

"Don't count on it," Brianne said.

I sat down on the floor, leaned against Dudley, and read the new-visitor form. It said all kinds of interesting stuff about our drooling guest. It said staying in new places makes Dudley nervous, so he drools more. Keeping him calm and quiet makes him drool less.

I got done reading and couldn't believe my eyeballs. My heart started to beat fast.

"Are you kidding me?" I cried. "Alfreeda, why didn't you tell me?"

"Huh?" She wrinkled her nose. "What?"

"Dudley's owners say he has great skateboard skills! They say if we have a skateboard, and the weather cools down, Dudley can show us his moves! Why didn't you *say* something?"

Alfreeda rolled her eyes. "Because it's *hot* outside," she said in her I'm-so-tired-of-explaining-things-to-my-dumb-brother voice.

"Well, we don't have to go outside," I said. "Dudley can skateboard inside, where it's cool. How about the hallway?"

"Right." Alfreeda rolled her eyes again. "Like Mom will go for that."

"I'll talk her into it," I said. "You know she'll do anything to make a dog happy. Dudley's stuck indoors on a hot day. Skateboarding is the most fun thing in the world for him. Mom will understand. For sure."

"I don't know." Alfreeda shook her head.

I jumped up. "I'll be right back."

"Where are you going?"

"To get my skateboard," I said. "*Finally* some fun for Dudley and me!"

I scrambled to the door, slipping and sliding on dog food and drool. And then . . . Mom, two Labrador retrievers, and three golden retrievers walked in.

Mom's mouth fell open. Her eyeballs almost popped out of her head.

"What on earth?" she cried. "What in the WORLD happened in here? ALFIE!"

CHAPTER 7
No Magic Wand

For the next couple of minutes, my life flashed before my eyes. Or maybe it was just a bunch of hairy dogs flashing past me. The retrievers dived at the food lying all over the floor. Their wild barking shook the walls.

"Sit! Stay! Play dead!" Mom commanded.

Not one of the dogs listened.

Alfreeda and I tried to help round them up. Brianne stood up and tried to help too. But we all kept slipping and sliding on Dudley's drool.

The other dogs were drooling now too, making more rivers on the floor. It's a simple fact of nature, I guess: The sight of food makes a dog drool like crazy.

Finally Mom yelled, "SIT!"

Mom never shouts in front of visitors, dog or human. You can bet we all paid attention. Even Alfreeda and I sat, right in the middle of two little drool lakes.

Sitting in wet jeans on top of dog food didn't feel so great. But I sure didn't say anything. I knew better.

Mom took a few deep breaths.

"Brianne," she said, "are you okay? You look like you had the wind knocked out of you."

Brianne nodded. "I took a little tumble earlier," she said, "but no harm done. If you don't need me for anything here, I think I'll head back to work."

"I am so, so sorry about this mess," Mom said, walking Brianne to the door. "Please call me later, and let me know how you're doing."

"Will do," Brianne said.

After Brianne left, Mom turned back to my sister. "Now . . . Alfreeda," she said, nearly whispering, "take the retrievers to their pens. Give them water. Put on calm, relaxing music. Close the blinds. If it's dark and quiet, maybe they'll nap."

"Sure, Mom," Alfreeda said.

She and the pack of dogs disappeared, like magic. Then the room got creepy quiet.

Mom stared at me. I swallowed hard.

"How could you let this happen, Alfie?" Mom asked. "Some new dog owners are coming to visit in less than an hour. They're going to tour the hotel. If they're happy with what they see, they'll become new customers. If not . . . Oh, Alfie, you *know* how much we need the business."

"Sorry, Mom." Spit caught in my throat, and I gagged a little.

"This room *must* be spotless before they arrive," Mom continued. "Get busy. Never before has a room needed to get clean so quickly. Understand?"

I nodded.

Mom hurried down the hall and disappeared into the kennel room.

When I turned around, I almost had to laugh. Dudley had climbed on the couch.

He sat upright, like a person. He looked like a hairy, wrinkly old grandpa.

His front leg rested on the arm of the couch. His other front leg rested on his knee. His back paws hung off the edge, just like an old man's slippers would.

His eyes were closed, but his mouth hung open. Strings of drool dripped out. Of course.

Then he started to snore. I think the office windows rattled.

I sighed and got to work.

🐾 🐾 🐾

The clean-up job took forEVER.

Mom kept coming in and checking on me. I'd say, "It's done!" And she'd say, "Not quite." She kept pointing out more messes that Dudley had made. Messes that *I* had to clean up.

"I see more dog food under that shelf. . . .

"Dudley licked the window. You need to wash that. . . .

"Dudley drooled on the chair pad. You need to wipe that. . . ."

When Mom left after the third check-up, I poked Dudley awake.

"Listen, dude," I whispered. "What's wrong with this picture? I'm spending too much time cleaning up after you. It's not like I have a magic wand I can wave around. Besides, I don't even believe in magic anymore. The messes around here just get worse! So listen up. We're not going to have ANY time for ANY fun today if you don't clean up your act, okay? So, come on. Help me out."

Dudley snored. He'd closed his eyes and fallen back to sleep.

To be honest I couldn't blame him. I knew how dumb I sounded. He was a *dog*, for Pete's sake. It was natural for him to make

messes. Just like it was natural for me. It's not something we could help, exactly. I thought about that for a minute, even though Dudley's loud snoring made it a little hard to think.

What we need to do, I told myself, *is keep these messes from happening in the first place.*

And I knew just how to do it.

I poked Dudley awake again and helped him off the couch. He walked all zigzaggy toward his pen.

"Hang in there, big guy," I said. "We've got just a little more work to do. Then we can get this party started. At last!"

CHAPTER 8
The Skateboard King

I ran up to the attic in our big farmhouse. I dug through boxes, tossing stuff left and right. Once I found what I was looking for, I raced back to Dudley's pen.

"You're a mess-making machine, Dudley," I said. "We're going to fix that."

I tied an old bib around his neck. I hung another one on the gate for a spare.

"This'll catch some of your drool," I said. "When this one is wet, we'll put the dry one on you. How's that sound?"

He woofed, quiet-like. I could tell he didn't want to wake the napping dogs.

"You're a dog with a big heart," I said. "And a dog who can't help making big messes."

He licked my face. It was a real spitty lick.

Next I gave him one of my worn-out stuffed animals, one I played with when I was a baby. He started to chew it right away.

"That's the idea," I said. "It'll act like a sponge for your spit. When that one gets full of drool, you can chew on another one." I pointed at the pile of old stuffed animals I'd brought from the attic.

Under Dudley's water bowl, I laid a big beach towel.

"Now we won't have to wipe the floor every time you take a drink," I said. "Cool, huh?"

Finally I waved Mom over. I showed her my ways to keep Drooling Dudley mess-free.

"That's great," she whispered. She hugged me and grinned. "This will cut the work in half, at least."

I decided to ask the pressing question. The one about skateboarding in the hallway.

"Well, maybe," she said. "After the new customers take their tour. And after the other dogs wake up. But first there's one last thing you need to clean."

"Aww, Mom. Now what?" I asked. "I've already cleaned *everything*!"

She leaned close and explained.

I quit complaining and got busy.

My final clean-up job was to wash Dudley's wrinkly face. Then I had to dry it super well.

Mom explained why: "The skin around a bulldog's mouth can get infected. It's from all the drooling. A bulldog's face should be washed with soap at least once a day."

I sure didn't want Dudley to get an infection, so I watched Mom close. She showed me how to wipe between the wrinkles, gently, with a soapy cloth.

Then I dried Dudley's face. After that, Mom and I put on powder and cream.

I made a chart to remind me to wash Dudley's face every day during his visit. I even drew a picture of a bulldog on it.

Once that was done, we two messy guys played — real quiet — with the beach ball until naptime ended.

When Mom gave the okay, naptime ended. I got out my skateboard. Alfreeda and I could hardly keep from jumping up and down.

"I can't believe Mom is letting us use the whole building, not just the hallway," I said. "It's like someone cast a magic spell on her."

"No kidding," Alfreeda said. "But she knows how much Dudley will love it. Mom is all about making the hotel guests happy!"

I set my board on the floor in the middle of the kennel room. Then Alfreeda opened Dudley's gate.

"Come on, boy!" I called, patting the board. "Show us your cool moves!"

I didn't have to ask twice. Dudley woofed and headed straight for the skateboard.

He set his left paws on the board and kept his right ones on the floor. He pushed off, and the board rolled super fast across the room. He pushed again and rode standing just on his left two legs. I couldn't believe it!

The skateboard bumped into a shelf and stopped. Dudley hopped off, turned around, and faced the other way. Now he stood on his right legs and pushed with his left.

He reached the kennel room door and leaned to the side. He made the skateboard turn the corner and head up the hallway.

"Man, did you see that?" I cried. "He can even turn corners!"

Alfreeda clapped and cheered. "Awesome! Go, Dudley!"

We ran after him. By the time we caught up, he had reached the office. The skateboard bumped into a potted plant and stopped. Dudley jumped off the board, picked it up with his mouth, and carried it back to the hallway. There he jumped on again and rode back to the kennel room.

The other dogs went crazy. They barked their heads off. It's like they were saying, "You're the Skateboard King, Dudley Bulldog!"

I totally agreed.

"Hey, how about we make a bridge with our arms?" I said. "Dudley can skateboard right under us."

"Cool," Alfreeda said. "And we could build a tunnel out of blankets. He could skateboard through it."

"Great idea!" I said.

Watching Dudley, I decided a dog this amazing shouldn't wear a baby bib. I took it off and put a Hound Hotel T-shirt on him to catch the drool. Alfreeda added sunglasses. He really looked cool.

"Smile, Dudley, you rockstar!" Mom said, taking his picture.

A few minutes later, she let the other dogs out into the play yard. Dudley had to stay inside. But I didn't feel bad for him. He just kept skateboarding like a pro, with Alfreeda and me chasing after him and cheering.

It felt like magic, I tell you. Yep, real magic.

Is an English Bulldog the Dog for You?

Hi! It's me, Alfreeda!

I bet you want your own sweet, loving English bulldog now too, right? Of course you do! English bulldogs are calm, friendly, gentle, and great with kids. They make good pets for many families, even though they snore, drool, and shed a lot.

But before you zoom off to buy or adopt one, here are some important facts you should know:

English bulldog puppies cost a lot of money. Because they have such large, square heads, bulldogs can't be born the natural way. Veterinarians have to bring them into the world by a special operation. Even with a vet's help, many bulldog puppies die at birth. (I know, it's very, very sad.)

English bulldogs don't live very long. They live only six to ten years. If that makes you too sad, you should get a pet that lives longer, like a turtle.

Most English bulldogs have health troubles. Some bulldogs have hip and knee pain. Some have heart, tail, or eye problems. Many have breathing problems. If your family can't pay for pricey trips to the vet, don't get a bulldog (or any dog). Get a goldfish instead.

Okay, signing off for now . . . until the next adventure at Hound Hotel!

Yours very factually,

Alfreeda Wolfe

VISIT
HOUND HOTEL
AGAIN WITH
THESE AWESOME
ADVENTURES!

Learn more about the people and pups of Hound Hotel
www.capstonekids.com

ADVENTURES AT HOUND HOTEL
Cool Crosby
WRITTEN BY Shelley Swanson Sateren
ILLUSTRATION BY Deborah Melmon

ADVENTURES AT HOUND HOTEL
Drooling Dudley
WRITTEN BY Shelley Swanson Sateren
ILLUSTRATION BY Deborah Melmon

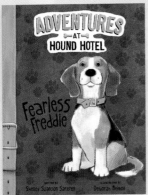

ADVENTURES AT HOUND HOTEL
Fearless Freddie
WRITTEN BY Shelley Swanson Sateren
ILLUSTRATION BY Deborah Melmon

ADVENTURES AT HOUND HOTEL
Growling Gracie
WRITTEN BY Shelley Swanson Sateren
ILLUSTRATION BY Deborah Melmon

ADVENTURES AT HOUND HOTEL
Homesick Herbie
WRITTEN BY Shelley Swanson Sateren
ILLUSTRATION BY Deborah Melmon

ADVENTURES AT HOUND HOTEL
Mighty Murphy
WRITTEN BY Shelley Swanson Sateren
ILLUSTRATION BY Deborah Melmon

ADVENTURES AT HOUND HOTEL
Mudball Molly
WRITTEN BY Shelley Swanson Sateren
ILLUSTRATION BY Deborah Melmon

ADVENTURES AT HOUND HOTEL
Stinky Stanley
WRITTEN BY Shelley Swanson Sateren
ILLUSTRATION BY Deborah Melmon

About the Author

Shelley Swanson Sateren grew up with five pet dogs — a beagle, a terrier mix, a terrier-poodle mix, a Weimaraner, and a German shorthaired pointer. As an adult, she adopted a lively West Highland white terrier named Max. Besides having written many children's books, Shelley has worked as a children's book editor and in a children's bookstore. She lives in Saint Paul, Minnesota, with her husband, and has two grown sons.

About the Illustrator

Deborah Melmon has worked as an illustrator for more than 25 years. After graduating from Academy of Art University in San Francisco, she started her career illustrating covers for the *Palo Alto Weekly* newspaper. Since then, she has produced artwork for more than 20 children's books. Her artwork can also be found on giftwrap, greeting cards, and fabric. Deborah lives in Menlo Park, California, and shares her studio with an energetic Airedale Terrier named Mack.